The Whisperin
A Horror Novella
Kay Parker

Also, by Kay Parker

Silvashire Chronicles Trilogy
Brooding and the Geek-A Prequel Short- (Coming Soon...)
Sleeping with Her Demons-Book One-
Standalone Novels and Novellas
The Whispering Woods
The VVitch (Coming March 2021)

To my Mother, L.
Thank you for introducing me to the Lost Boys and Hellraiser at an age that was probably inappropriate but greatly appreciated. You made me the horror junkie I am today.
I love you, Doe.

"If you go down to the woods today you better go run and hide, if you go down to the woods today you better clutch your crucifix tight...For today's the day the Ghastling wants her picnic..."

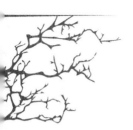

Chapter One

My name is Lucinda Porter and I wish that the tale I am about to tell you was not my own. Unfortunately, I was there, and I saw the horrors that I am going to share with you now with my own eyes. Felt them with my own hands. Lived through them with my own body. I lost my friends to the horrors, my family and many would say I also lost my mind. I wouldn't agree to the last one, but they do say the mad never believe themselves to be insane, so maybe they're right and I am wrong. Somehow... I don't think that's correct.

Where should I begin my tale? Here, now, where I am sat in a corner of a dusty, white room in the Posybrooke Asylum for the Mentally Unhinged? Or perhaps when I was born a lonely, only-child to a small family in the darkest, unknown valleys of England? None of these places seem right. So maybe the best start is when I started to notice that something was wrong? Yes. That's the right place. Let me begin...

ONE MORNING LIKE ANY other I went to meet my friends, Casey, Lola and Teddy in the woods near my home. A dark and tangled woodland which was as old as the hills themselves. We did this most days without much trouble but today was going to be much, much different. When I arrived at our usual meeting spot Casey and Lola were crying and angry. Teddy was watching them with a gleeful yet anxious look on his face. We were still at the age where making girls cry was a small triumph for Teddy, much like the small feeling of joy we girls had when

3

Teddy was poked fun at for 'playing with girls'. Not yet adults but no longer children, we were at the twilight place in-between. Thinking about that, maybe that's why things became so different from that day. Maybe our state of in-between drew it to us? But I am losing my thread. The girls were crying, and I found I was quite shaken at the sight of Teddy in the face of such torment. I jumped from my bicycle and stomped over to Teddy, shoving him, and demanding, "What the hell is going on? What did you do, Ted?"

Teddy glared at me, "I just told them about the Ghastling, just the Ghastling," he told me defiantly. He didn't want to admit that I could beat him if it came to a fight, my tendencies to step out of the carefully curated box that is marked 'female' has always bothered him. Teddy was a good kid. Tall, gangly and slim with brown posh boy hair and always wearing round glasses and button up shirts. He was known as the pretty boy and for this reason was often the ridicule of the other boys who I always suspected where more jealous of him than they cared to admit. On the other hand, I was a petite girl with long, loose honey-coloured hair, a fashion that was more suited to Teddy's grandma, with a book permanently in my backpack yet a tendency to cuss like a sailor and fight anyone who breached my sense of right and wrong. Casey and Lola were twins. Pretty things with baby blonde curls that Casey wore in a high ponytail and Lola wore cut into a curly bob. They were all pretty dresses and perfectly painted nails, and I had a feeling that Lola went with it more to suit Casey and her mother than because she actually liked it. She was always the first of us to dive into any sticky situation, the first to get her hands dirty and the only one who threw a punch beside me. I loved her fiercely, but back then I didn't know that. Back then I thought those feelings were just how we felt because we were best friends. I didn't realise we weren't like other girls until much later.

All this to say that Teddy was used to my shoves and occasional thumps and he resented them with a smile rather than ever shove me back. Barbed words were his method of retaliation when he felt it was required. I looked squarely at him now with a sceptical look, "The Ghastling? Where did you hear that?" I scoffed. It was then that Lola spoke up, wiping her eyes and scowling at Teddy she said, "Teddy said that his brother had told him about a strange, scary demonic creature called The Ghastling that lives in these woods and feeds on the souls of its victims."

"He said that we've spent so much time in these woods that it's bound to know us and be biding its time to tear us limb from limb," Casey added with a whimper.

I looked from the girls to Teddy and back then let out a sigh, "It's tosh, Teddy and you know it so why scare them?" I was angry because I knew the story of the Ghastling, and it wasn't a nice tale. It was local folklore that anyone within Posybrooke knew from birth, but Casey and Lola had only moved her a year before and didn't know the tale. It was a partially true story and that made it much worse, I didn't know then that the stories that came after were true too. I flipped Teddy the bird and linked arms with the girls, "come on, lets go!" I told them as I lead them away. Teddy didn't try to stop us. He just watched us wander deeper into the woods with that anxious look on his face, thinly veiled by his own anger.

I led the girls towards the stream at the centre of the woods and we sat on a rotted fallen log and watched the water insects skittering along leaving ripples and whirls on the black, brackish water. Lola picked up a rock and tried to skim it long the stream but instead it landed with a watery plop. We exchanged a smile and our eyes turned in unison to Casey where she sat still weeping quietly.

"Case? It's just a stupid story, don't cry," Lola said with a voice trying and failing to sound sympathetic. I held my tongue about the fact it was a stupid story based very much on fact and instead wrapped my arms around Casey with a dramatic sigh and squeezed her.

"Oh! Casey! Casey! Cheer your face up. Teddy just wants to scare you because he has the romantic tact of a jellyfish. You know he has a crush you; we know he has a crush on you. This is his idea of making you interested," I told her, pulling my silliest faces as I did so. Casey wiped her eyes and laughed and nodded her agreement. Lola threw her arms around us both and we all laughed. It was blissful and we felt all the happiness and carefree cheer in those years between childhood and adulthood. That is before the Ghastling...

Before the whispering woods began to *Whisper*...

THINGS AT THIS POINT began to show the first stirrings of getting strange. We didn't know then that this was the start of a whole great nightmare for us, but it was. The stream began to *TALK* to us, a deep, rattling, grating moan of a voice whispering in a harsh, violent rasp... It said, "*If you go down to the woods today you better go run and hide, if you go down to the woods today you better clutch your crucifix tight...For today's the day the Ghastling wants her picnic...*" It sang this on repeat, over and over as we sat huddled together on that mouldy log with eyes like saucers, listening.

We didn't move until Casey screamed. Then we ran as fast as we could back towards where we'd left our bikes. Back towards where we'd left Teddy, hoping against all hope that he had waited for us. The woods whispering their grotesque rhyme all around us as we crashed from the trees and into the clearing where our bikes lay in dirt. Teddy was gone. His bike was not.

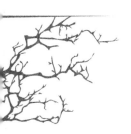

Chapter Two

The next few hours flew by in a blur of worried parents, police officers and endless cups of tea being shoved our way by kind strangers. We sat huddled together in the folds of an orange and brown quilted blanket on Mrs Weatherman's cat scented sofa whilst the police and our parents helped Teddy's mum look for him well into the night. Mrs Weatherman was my elderly next-door neighbour, she was friends with my mum and sent me cards and cat shaped gifts each birthday and Christmas since I could remember. She'd always been old, even when I was a toddler running round with sticky fingers and a snotty nose. She must have been about one hundred now, but she fussed and ran around for us like we were the ones with crippling arthritis and cataracts. Casey and Lola slept at intervals on the sofa beside me, but I couldn't unwind enough to drop off, my mind raced with various grisly images of what could have happened to Teddy. Mrs Weatherman dozed in her armchair by the fire with a book in her lap. I wanted to take it and see what she was reading but Lola's head rested on my shoulder and I didn't want to disturb her. I glanced at the cat shaped plastic clock on the wall, it's eyes ticking with each second and its eyes looking side to side as if it was also looking for Teddy. It was three in the morning, the last thing I saw before falling into a restless sleep was those horrible, glancing cat eyes.

Tick...tick.... ticking.

THE NEXT DAY WAS NO better. We woke to more sugary tea and gooey blueberry muffins and the sound of Mrs Weatherman's various cats mewling for their breakfast in the kitchen. We nibbled the muffins and sipped the tea and sat in silence watching the window, waiting for our parents to return and tell us Teddy was found and safe and all was well. Still, we were hopeful that this was all just silly misunderstanding. No one came and we were still with Mrs Weatherman at dinner time. Casey was asleep again, curled up in the orange and brown quilt after a fit of crying had left her exhausted. Lola was sat by the window playing with Mrs Weatherman's newest cat, a small kitten named Treacle with mottled black and beige fur and mismatched eyes. I sat at Lola's feet with my paperback sometimes reading and sometimes daydreaming, but mostly just watching Lola. Mrs Weatherman bought us all fish and chips for dinner, and we ate around her kitchen table from the newspaper they came wrapped in. Mrs Weatherman said it tasted better out of the newspaper, but we were just so hungry that even the greasy newspaper would have tasted good to us. None of us had spoken since we arrived with Mrs Weatherman and I now felt that breaking the silence to thank her for the dinner would be somehow disturbing some unushered rule, like breaking the silence would damn Teddy in some way. So, despite knowing better, I remained silent and the girls remained silent except for when Casey cried herself into another sleep.

DAY THREE ARRIVED AND went on much as the day before and the day before that. Still, none of us spoke and still Mrs Weatherman fussed and pampered us and by dinner time we were all quite comfortable when a knock at the door disturbed our cosy silence. My mum had returned weary, cold and tired to collect us and take us home. She told us, "Teddy is nowhere to be found and there is no trace of him. The po

ce are going to continue the search but have sent Miss Nicholls home
with Mr and Mrs Finch, so she isn't alone. The girls are going to stay with
s for a few days whilst she settles, okay?" We listened, blinked a few
imes and gave uncertain nods of the head and agreeing sounds. Teddy
was nowhere to be found. The words clanged in my skull like the stat-
: of an old TV and sent chills down my spine. Casey cried again as we
limbed the steps to my house.

We needed to help Teddy somehow, I felt a nagging tug inside that
old me that perhaps we could find him because we knew his hideouts
nd safe places better than anyone. That night as I was tucked up in my
ed with Lola curled into my side and Casey laid on the pull-out be-
ow us, I told them my plan. "In the morning we're going to find Teddy.
We know where he was that night before we left. We weren't gone long
nough for him to go far, and we know the woods better than anyone.
We have to find him," I told them in whispers, so my mum didn't hear
s. Lola nodded her head once with a determined and steely look in her
yes. Casey was less certain but wouldn't dream of turning her back on
ny of us—least of all Teddy. "That's settled then, we head out first thing
nd we find him," I smiled.

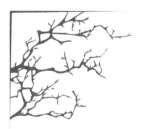

Chapter Three

Let me pause a moment now to tell you about the legend of th Ghastling that was so popular amongst young children and gangl teens in my village. The tale goes that deep in the whispering woods o dark evenings between dust and dark if you listen carefully, you will hea the woods whisper songs of the Ghastling. It is said that those who hea these songs are the chosen ones, the ones who the Ghastling is going t come for next, creeping, skulking and writhing her way through th woods to find you and sip your eyeballs through your skull, crunch you bones and devour your soul. It has been local lore for as long as the wood had people living around them and maybe even before then too. Fact mingled into the lore, perhaps afterwards or perhaps at the beginning No one really knows; but there is an old husk of a cottage in the wood almost nothing left but the floorboards rotting and mildewed, and th cobblestone walls covered in lichen and moss. It's known to locals as th Ghastling's hovel but in reality, it was the home of an elderly woman wh owned the land in the early days of the village, she was thought a witch b the few yokels living in the early village and they burned her alive outsid her own home when a child went missing in the woods. They believe she had taken him and eaten him. I do not know, not even now, if thi was true or if they had murdered an innocent old woman for being sim ply old and alone. However, her story became interwoven with that o the Ghastling—one and the other the same—and no one went near th remains of the cottage and children still went missing in the woods al these years later.

No one much minded the legend, no one really took much notice o it and it was usually used as a little catch for visitors to the village or b older kids to scare their siblings and friends. Just Halloween dares and campfire scares that everyone knew and never paid much attention to. I'd never paid attention to it even though I knew that the old woman from the cottage had been real, even though my mum—an historian—had researched the woman and I had seen her research and KNEW that at least half of the legend had really, actually happened. I still didn't believe in the Ghastling. Except now Teddy had gone missing in the woods and the whispering, ratting rhyme we heard that day kept playing in my mind over and over again and I was beginning to wonder if I had been wrong to dismiss the rest of the tale with such certainty. I was beginning to wonder 'what if...?' and I was beginning to worry that we'd never see Teddy again.

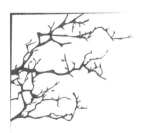

Chapter Four

That next day we returned to the opening in the woods where we usually met. The place we had last seen Teddy and where his bike still lay in the dirt, surrounded now by police tape and the odd bouquet of sickly, sweet, decaying flowers. Casey let out a loud choking sob at the sight and buried her face into Lola's shoulder. Lola hushed her absent-mindedly whilst staring wild eyed at the bouquets.

"They're beginning to think he's dead, aren't they?" Lola muttered half to herself. I nodded and leaned down by the bike, feeling in the dirt for any sign of Teddy and knowing before I started that I'd find nothing. I looked up towards the stream where we had heard the woods whisper their horrid rhyme and then around the opening again. The only other path besides the one we took to the stream was the one into the wild-wood, deeper in the woods where the oaks grew fat and strong. If he'd stuck to the path, then that's the only place he could have gone. I threw my leg back over my bike and headed down the path. I heard Casey and Lola moving around in the leaves behind me before they followed. We didn't speak again until we reached the great oak at the end of the long, winding path. The path to the oaks was a solid three mile walk but didn't take very long at full speed on our bikes. The police had searched here too, we could tell by the many, haphazard boot prints all over the ground. The police didn't know about the hollow oak though, the one we used as our woodland hideout. I dropped my bike by the great oak and waited for Lola and Casey. Together we climbed over the small wooden fencing that surrounded the edge of the path and ventured into the woods. Just off the path to the left of the great oak was the hollow oak, a wide

ollowed out tree hidden from anyone passing by. Our woodland club-
ouse.

WAS BOTH DISAPPOINTED and surprised when we entered the
ollow oak and found Teddy was not there. I flopped down onto the
ld, stained and moulding duvet that we used as flooring inside the oak
nd huffed a sigh. "If he didn't come to the hollow oak, where would he
ave gone?" I asked no one in particular. Lola shrugged and sat down be-
de me, dropping her head softly onto my shoulder. I looked at Casey
·ho was ferreting around in the crate by the opening of the hollow oak.
·What's up Case?" I called to her. She beckoned me over with her pret-
·y polished hand so together myself and Lola got up and headed across.
·asey had found Teddy's glasses; they were cracked, and one arm was
·roken as if they'd be trodden on. My face blanched and Lola let out a
·w whistle. "Shit..." I whispered.

"Teddy is literally blind as a bat without his glasses and he's been
·one **FOUR DAYS**. There's no way he could get around for four days
·ithout his glasses, Lu..." Casey said softly, her eyes were full of tears and
· could tell she was on the verge of another crying fit. I nodded slowly
·nd glanced at Lola; she was staring into the woods with a strange look
·n her face.

"Lola?" I said. Lola didn't respond, she didn't even blink. She just
·ared out into the woods. "Lola? What is it?" I said again, louder this
· me. Lola tilted her head and wandered towards the spot she was staring
· . "Lola? Talk to us!" I snapped, the anxiety and fear making me cranky.
·ola held up her hand as if to tell me to shut up, so I did and slowly I fol-
·wed her, Casey close behind me. As we approached the spot Lola was
·eading for, we noticed what she had seen. I heard Casey gasp a sob be-
·ind me and I reached my hand back to grab hers, giving it a squeeze.

She squeezed back as we stopped beside Lola and stared down at a thick pool of rancid blood, thick and clumpy like it was starting to dry up with a scrap of Teddy's shirt tangled in the twigs and leaves amongst it. I bent down slowly and reached out my hand to pluck the fabric from the drying pool but as I did, so the trees began to whisper.

"*If you go down to the woods today you better go run and hide. If you go down to the woods today, you'd better clutch your crucifix tight. For today's the day the Ghastling wants her picnic...*" the trees sang in their twisted, ghastly whispering voice. Over and over and over. I froze and felt Lola tense beside me. Casey let out a low whimper and we all looked around slowly. Exchanging glances now and again as the trees whispered all around us. "Do...do you think she's real?" Casey asked.

"It's just a story, a dumb story," Lola said with a harsh tone, her fear obvious in that very tone because Lola never snapped at Casey, ever.

"I think we need to be open to anything right now," I said truthfully. It was then that the thing happened that finally made us realise that things had become very different for us, that life would never be the same again. A horrible, bone-chilling screech echoed all around us and we turned as one towards the sound to see...*HER*... She stood between the trees with her bare feet, bloodied and dirty. An old, once-white gown hung from her body in rags, revealing one bare leg to the thigh and hanging from one shoulder by the tatters of a strap, the other side torn and mostly missing, revealing a bloodied and emancipated chest and one dirty, bloodied breast. She was baring her yellowed, blood crusted teeth and her where her eyes should be were hollowed out bloodied holes dripping down her cheeks. Hair matted and tangled on top of her head. She raised her head and screeched again and as she did, we saw deep in the gory holes where her eyes belonged a strange white glow. Casey screamed, pushed me aside and ran deeper into the woods.

"Casey no!!" Lola screamed after her, but she didn't leave me. She pulled me to my feet and checked I could run before turning to follow her sister. I looked towards the Ghastling to see she was gone. Fear melt d into a puddle inside me and I gripped Lola's hand, jerking her back to ιe. "What is it?" she said frantically, glancing back and forth between ιe and the woods where Casey had fled.

"She's gone..." I whispered, pointing to the empty space where the ;hastling had stood. We then heard a strangled cry, a screech and then lence. "Case!?" I yelled at the top of my lungs. "Casey?!" Lola grabbed ιy hand and together we ran through the woods, following Casey's :acks in the dirt until we came to another puddle of blood. This one wet ιd warm and holding Casey's severed eyeball....

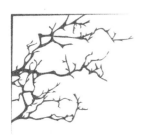

Chapter Five

I don't remember now how we got home, how we told my mum about Casey, or how I comforted Lola as she screamed and cried for a week afterwards. I only know these things happened because my mum told me so, later on when things began to feel normal again. My memories of the few weeks and months after the Ghastling took Casey are sporadic and hazy. I remember police being everywhere. I remember they believed Teddy and Casey were the victims of some deranged paedophile and murderer and I remember the village getting a curfew enforced for all under eighteens. I recall Lola was always at my house after Casey had gone and our relationship had somehow developed in those few hazy months before my seventeenth birthday. I remember realising my feelings for Lola were not normal, friendship feelings but actually love of the romantic kind. I remember our first tearful kiss. I remember Mr and Mrs Finch getting a divorce, unable to get past the loss of their dear, sweet Casey and not being present enough to care about the effect this would all have on Lola, their remaining child. I recall Mr Finch moving away and never seeing him again. I also remember Mrs Finch overdosing on sleeping pills when Lola stayed over one night. I remember it resulted in my mum letting Lola move in with us permanently, and how Lola was more excited about that than she was upset by the loss of her mother. Miss Nicholl moved away shortly after, the loss of her best friend so close to the loss of her only son was too much and she returned home to her own mother. All these things I remember with the misty haze of seeing them happen in slow motion through frosted glass. Like I'm watching someone else's memories rather than recalling my own. Nothing from those few months is clear, not until Mrs Weatherman.

IT HAD BEEN ABOUT FIVE months since Casey had been taken, my seventeenth birthday had been and gone and Lola's seventeenth was fast approaching. There was two months between our birthdays, mine the thirteenth of June and Lola's the thirteenth of August, only three days away. We were sat in the living room on my mum's battered old floral sofa reading *Star Wars* comics to each other and drinking spiked mugs of coffee with whipped cream. My mum was working long shifts at the library researching her latest book. There was a knock on the door and Mrs Weatherman stood there with a bright pink box tied with a yellow bow. "Hello, Mrs Weatherman, are you okay?" I smiled at her warmly. I loved Mrs Weatherman even if she was a nosy little crazy cat lady and possibly a zombie considering she just kept on living despite being impossibly old.

"Oh! Me? I'm fine lovey. It's little Lola's birthday this weekend I hear, so I thought I'd pop her a gift around before I leave," Mrs Weatherman smiled at me as she handed over the brightly coloured box.

I took the box and smiled back, "going south for the winter, Mrs Weatherman?" I asked with a chuckle; however, her reply knocked the smile clean off my face and left me gaping at the door like a fish out of water.

"Oh no lovey. The Ghastling's coming for me, I've got an appointment that can't be missed to be with my beloved Floyd again," with that she shuffled back towards her house. Lola came up behind me and gripped my shoulder.

"What did she just say?" she asked in a tone that told me she knew very well what Mrs Weatherman had just said. I turned to her and took in the faraway, pained look in her eyes and handed her the box. We sat on the edge of the sofa and Lola gingerly untied the bow and opened the lid, inside the box was cat shaped purse with bright green eyes and glittery whiskers. We both sighed in unison, relief palpable that it wasn't something sinister. Then Lola picked up the purse and as she did something rattled in the box. Removing the tissue paper Lola gasped. Inside the box was Casey's charm bracelet, the one she was wearing the day she was taken. A silver linked chain with daisy and gem charms.

"How the hell did she get this?" Lola almost screamed.

"I don't know, but we should go check on her," I said as I headed back to the front door. Lola followed me and we headed towards Mrs Weatherman's next door when I caught sight of her crossing into the woods down the street. "Shit! Come on!" I said to Lola and I jogged down the road towards Mrs Weatherman. She vanished into the trees before we reached her and although we looked around for the rest of the day, we never found Mrs Weatherman. By nightfall we were forced to return home and wait for mum, but no one ever saw Mrs Weatherman again. The only thing they ever found was her bloodied, cat print apron. As she had been an elderly woman, they didn't link her disappearance to those of Teddy or Casey. The police wrote her disappearance off as an accident due to advanced age. Although Lola and I knew better, we knew that Mrs Weatherman was the third victim to be taken by the Ghastling that year and time was running out.

"WHAT ARE WE GOING TO do?" Lola asked me that night as we laid in bed listening to the rain pitter patter on the roof. The bedroom was dark, and the curtains were slightly open, so the moonlight lit up a slice of the bed where we lay. I rolled over in bed to face her and shook my head.

"I'm not sure but we need to do something to stop this before someone else gets taken," I said, mulling the events over in my mind. Playing back again that horrible rhyme over and over again in my mind. I looked t the ceiling. The moonlight glowed just enough for me to see the wind-harm above my bed slowly swaying like a baby's mobile. I watched it in n almost hypnotised fashion for several minutes as I mulled over the ays in which we could somehow help stop the Ghastling, lost in the way of the feathered charms as they twirled and flowed in the slight reeze. I felt Lola's breath against my cheek, but she remained quiet, aiting for me to suggest something. By the time I'd come up with a lausible yet dangerous plan she had fallen asleep.

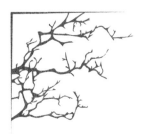

Chapter Six

I was making pancakes the next morning in the open plan kitchen m
mum was so proud of. The scent of creamy pancake batter and citrus
sweet oranges filled the air and the scent lead Lola from the bedroom i
search of the delicious aroma. When she saw me stood by the kitche
sink with a plate of pancakes and batter on my face, she smiled a brigh
open smile. I hadn't seen that smile since the day Casey had died and t
finally see it again made my heart throb with a sharp pain of emotion
"Pancakes are up," I smiled back around the lump forming in my throat.

Lola sat at the table and began pouring juice onto her plate of pan
cakes with gusto. The sugar sat untouched—Lola liked her pancake
without—but Casey had always liked sugar and I was still in the habit o
putting it out for her, I suppose. I prepared my own pancakes and sat a
the table across from her. We ate in silence. When we finished eating,
decided to make my suggestion. "Lola? I have an idea, but you aren't go
ing to like it," I told her. Lola eyed me over her mug of tea, but she re
mained silent.

"I think we should go into the woods, to the Ghastling hovel and tr
to summon her to us. The rhyme...it says something about a crucifix s
maybe that harms her? Maybe we can use it against her?"

Lola's eyes widened and she spat her tea all over the table in he
shock, "are you kidding me right now? After what she did to Casey! Yo
want to look for the bitch?!" she hissed at me.

"We need to stop this, Lola. Before someone else gets hurt. Isn't i
enough? I thought it was over... Now Mrs Weatherman is gone!" I crie
My exasperation plain on my face as I scoffed at her. I understood her ap
prehension but didn't feel like it was helpful, nor acceptable at this mo

ent in time. I slammed my fist onto the table and stood up, shovelling
he pots into the sink with a clatter. "Who needs to die next before you'll
want to help? My mum? Me? YOU? We're the only ones left that haven't
ft or been taken and no one believes our story. They think we're un-
inged. Only we can stop her, Lola," I shouted frantically. Lola stared at
he with a hard contempt in her eyes that pained me, but I needed to be
dunt, needed to be cruel to be kind.

"You're a fucking piece of work, Lu. You know that?" Lola snarled.
he then shoved herself from the table and walked out. I never saw her
gain after that day. Not for a long while.

. FEW OF DAYS PASSED before I realised that Lola had left for good.
waited for her by the bay window of the living room for three days and
ights before I slowly began to lose hope. My mum had called around the
eighbours looking for her, but no one knew where she was, and no one
ad seen her. We tried calling her several times, but she kept hanging up
nd wouldn't talk to either of us. I suppose she was too ashamed of hurt-
ng my mum to talk to her, but I knew she didn't talk to me because she
vas mad and wanted to hurt me. As upset as I was by that knowledge, I
vas also relieved that she was hanging up our calls, that meant she was
afe. The Ghastling hadn't taken her.

By the end of the week my mum came to the conclusion that Lola
idn't want to come back and we began to clear out her things and box
hem up in the attic. It was a difficult time for me, but I knew that it
neant Lola might be safe, if she had left the village, she would be out of
he Ghastling's reach. At the end of the day as my mum made us hot co-
oa and we sat on the floor by the fireplace she let me in on a secret she'd
een keeping since before Lola left us.

"Lu, I'm taking a new job in London for a few weeks."

I looked at her in mild disbelief, then shook my head, "you're leavin, me alone? Really?"

"I need to take the job, Lu. It will mean big things for us. It's only few weeks and I'll be back home. You don't mind, right?" Mum said des perately. She wanted this so much I could tell that, but she was also no willing to hurt me—especially not now. I sighed.

"No, mum. I don't mind. The quiet might do me some good," forced a smile and she smiled back. We sipped our cocoa in silence an lost ourselves in our own thoughts for a few hours before we gave up an went to bed.

That night I couldn't sleep so I tried to find a silver lining in all tha happened. Lola was gone but she was safe, Mum was leaving but woul also be safe... Maybe now would be the perfect time to try and stop th Ghastling before mum returned? I considered the idea. Turning it ove and over in mind and weighing up the pros and cons, eventually I ha some crude form of plan and knew what I was going to do. As soon a Mum left, I was going hunting.

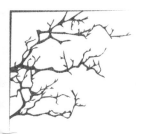

Chapter Seven

It was of course a few more days before my mum finally left for London, and in that time, things went slowly from bad to worse. I didn't know that at the time, but I found out as soon as I set off to find *her*...

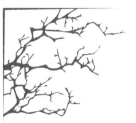

Chapter Eight

I found myself in the woods when I awoke. I was so cold I could see my breath like fog and my fingers would hardly move. I tried to curl my toes, but I couldn't feel my feet. Fear gripped me like a vice, and I felt a curl of panic in my chest. It was dark. Full dark. I didn't know where I was or how I had ended up here. My mind was a frozen blank. I could hear crickets and nocturnal animals scuffling around and I strained my ears to hear if anything else was amongst them. When I felt safe enough, I slowly sat up and found I was wrapped in my own woollen blankets and sleeping bag. Relief flooded me. I'd come into the woods looking for the Ghastling, to begin my hunt. I must have been more tired than I knew to awaken so disoriented. I rubbed my frozen fingers together and gave a small cough to break the silence. I pulled my blankets tighter around me and closed my eyes. Soon I was back asleep.

WHEN I WOKE AGAIN THE sun was high in the sky and I opened my eyes to see the treetops and flashes of blue sky between the leaves. I was much warmer, and I stretched my arms up above my head with a smile at the feeling of comfort. I rolled over in my sleeping bag and pushed myself up, as I looked around, I saw a trail of blood leading away from where I was sat. "Hello...?" I called. I felt braver in the daylight, so I slowly stood up and began to follow the trail. "Hello...?" I called again. The trail stopped with a matted, gooey pool of blood and signs of a struggle. I bent down and touched my fingers to the blood; it was cold but still

icky as if it wasn't too old. I looked around, saw a campfire still slightly
urning, a spilt mug of what looked like cocoa, a book and.... My back-
ack. I looked back the way I had come to where the only sign of my stay
as my blankets and sleeping bag. I reached slowly up to feel my face and
ead and my hands came away with crusts of mud and dried blood. "Shit.
hit, shit, shit, fucking shit! What happened?!" I hissed to myself in fear,
anic and confusion. I grabbed my backpack and ran back towards my
eeping bag. I needed to get as far away from this spot as possible and
y to figure out what or who had attacked me. My mind was still a fuzzy
lank and I felt sick with worry. If it had been her then surely, I'd be dead,
ght? So, who had attacked me and left me?

HAVE TO ADMIT NOW, looking back on it that I should have
nown that it could have been no one else. If I had been attacked by a
erson they wouldn't have just given up and left me, or if they did, they'd
ave stolen my belongings. Yet nothing was taken. However, the fear of
actually being her made my insides liquify so I could have just been
n denial. Either way, I soon found out just who it was. I gathered up
y things and headed deeper into the woods. I hadn't been walking long
hen I came across something in the leaves. Bending down to dig it out
ent a wave of dizziness through me, but I scooped up the fabric. It was
pink Aran sweater. Lola's. Nausea floored me and I collapsed to the
round clutching the jumper to my chest. I shook as the sobs wracked
e, "that bitch! I'll kill her," I cried. This changed everything. This was
o longer a hunt for facing a childhood nightmare, it was a hunt for
engeance, and I meant for my revenge to be served ice cold.

I stood on shaking legs and brushed dirt and leaves from my knees
ith a trembling hand before stuffing Lola's jumper into my bag and fish-
g out my carving knife. I had no idea if weapons would work against

something like the Ghastling, but I didn't want to do this empty handed either. My plans I knew were half-baked, but they were better than going in blind. Although, looking back I was as blind as they come.

With a mixture of fear and anger in my gut I headed towards the Ghastling's Hovel. I would face her there where I could use walls to prevent her sneaking up from behind, claws lashing and mouth snarling at my back. I would not let her catch me unguarded again.

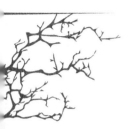

Chapter Nine

The old house at the centre of the deep woods was an old cobble-stone number, walls made with big grey rocks exposed indoors and ut, green moss and lichen growing over every inch of them. The win-ows that remained were mottled with mould and frosted with grime, so : was nearly impossible to see through them. The floor was matted with reeds and debris of leaves, dead birds and twigs. If there was ever a wood ooring in place it had long ago rotted away. I looked around at the de-aying pieces of furniture dotted around. It seemed someone had re-oved a lot of the long-ago owner's belongings, but some remained even ll these years later and made the cottage even more eerie. Like she would alk back through the door any moment. I shuddered at the thought. he cottage originated from the time before electricity so there were no seful lamps to light the rooms as dusk approached but luckily, I had an-icipated this and had candles in my bag. I got them out now and placed hem along the windowsills, lighting them as I went.

The place was deathly quiet, and I didn't break the silence, just lis-ened to the leaves rustle under my feet and the trees swish and whoosh utside in the wind. As darkness fell, I made up a bed on the old mould-ig sofa, pulled out my battered and slightly muddied paperback and set-led into my vigil for the night. I knew she might not approach right way or even at all. She might wait until I fall asleep or lead me into a alse sense of security then attack in several nights time. I had no idea ow she worked or what level of sentience or intelligence she had. All I ould do was wait.

I must have fallen asleep because the sound of whispering pulled me nto consciousness. Rubbing my eyes, I looked around; my book was

closed in my lap and the candles around the room were flickering in th
draught but all still lit. I tried to get to my feet, but the circulation ha
cut off in my legs whilst I had slept cross legged and as I rose from the so
fa the numbness turned to painful tingling and I fell to my knees with
grunt. I rubbed my legs with my hands to get the circulation going, angr
at myself for falling asleep and for letting my guard down. As the tinglin
subsided, I heard the whispering again…

*"If you go down to the woods today you better go run and hide. If you g
down to the woods today, you'd better clutch your crucifix tight. For today
the day the Ghastling wants her picnic…"*

Panic flooded me and I scrabbled to my feet and felt around me.
couldn't find the knife. I searched the sofa frantically and finally my han
fell on its sharp blade. I hissed as I slid my finger down it in my searc
and snatched it up as blood welled from the paper-thin cut. Spinning t
face the door I raised the knife. My heart pounded in my chest so fas
that I was sure the Ghastling would be able to hear it. The woods con
tinued their grim song all around me and it felt like the room had gotte
colder. I realised I was shaking and steeled my spine, faked a confidenc
I was far from feeling and tried to hear anything beyond the whisperin
trees and the winds. Suddenly a thud and a scrape behind me sounde
out and I yelped in fear. There stood a small door set into the wall tha
I hadn't noticed before, the scraping seemed to be coming from behin
it. "Rats?" I wondered aloud and stepped closer, rapping my knuckles o
the door.

"Someone help me!?" a grating woman's voice screamed back at me.

"Hello?" I called back, "are you okay? I'll get you out." I fumble
with the door, the door handle was jammed and wouldn't budge. "I
there anything in there you can use to prise the door?" I asked.

Scuffling and scraping noises sounded out and finally the woma
called, "no, nothing. She's left nothing in here but me."

"Stay back," I called and sacrificed my knife to free her. I slid th
blade between the door and jamb and hammered it deeper with the hee

of my palm. Once I felt it was deep enough, I wiggled the knife back and forth, back and forth until the door creaked, and the wood split against my blade. At last, the door made a loud cracking sound and the door slid open as I wiggled the blade. I pulled it quickly back and reached inside to pull the woman out. Her hands gripped my arm and wrist desperately and together we released her to freedom.

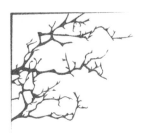

Chapter Ten

"Lu?! Oh gods...Lu! I thought I'd never see you again!" the woman cried throwing her arms around me and holding me tightly. She was bedraggled, bloodied and her hair in matted knots of grime and blood. I petted her back absentmindedly whilst scanning the room for signs of danger. The trees had whispered her coming and they never lied. "Lu...?" the woman said, more softly and a touch apprehensively this time. I looked down at her into familiar dusky eyes in an oval shaped face I knew better than my own.

"Lola? Is it really you?" I gasped as recognition dawned on me. She wasn't dead, she was captive. She was right here in my arms. I allowed myself a moment of joy and scanned her face for cuts or bruises before the reality of the situation slowly slotted into place. "She set you as bait to get me here..." I whispered, "she wants us both and now I've put us both in danger."

Lola sobbed, collapsing in on herself and clearly exhausted from her experience. She didn't appear to me wounded except for superficial cuts and grazes so I collected my knife and began searching for the Ghastling. There were no more hidden doors within the house so she would be coming from outside, I peered out of the window by the door and scanned the trees for signs of movement. They were quite now, but I had a feeling that didn't mean our safety—just that they knew I knew she was coming.

Behind me I heard Lola's muffled voice, "what will she do to us...?"

Turning to her I gave a small shrug, "nothing if I have anything to do with it. I'm going to stop her." Lola nodded but still looked troubled and I knew she didn't believe me, if I had any sense of my own, I would have known myself that I was talking nonsense. Sadly, we all think we're invinible at that age. I pulled Lola into my arms and rested my head on hers, try not to think about it, Lola. I'll get us out of here."

VE HAD BEEN RESTING like this for a few minutes when things took a turn for the worst. The trees began thrashing and whispering, although they whispered too quietly for me to hear the words, I knew they were singing that gods awful song. Lola whimpered as I stood and glanced out of the window, outside the trees were swaying like the winds were going 80mph yet nothing else moved. Then slowly, almost as if she was melting into existence the Ghastling appeared between the trees. Looking right at me.

Terrified I stumbled back from the window and landed heavily on my back with a thud, the knife skittered from my hand and vanished underneath the old sofa. I looked to where the knife had flown but couldn't see it, then my eyes roved over the window and she was there with her hideous, gnarled and bloodied face pressed against the glass. Her glowing hollow pits of eyes watching me, boring into me and freezing me in place. I couldn't move. Couldn't make a sound. I just lay there frozen in terror as my breath came in ragged gasps and my heart pounded in my ears.

"Lu?" Lola hissed from her hiding place behind the sofa. I was unable to utter a word of warning and she couldn't see what I was seeing. The door creaked open and the Ghastling stood there, deformed body covered in muck, grime and blood. Her ghastly wounds open and oozing as if she had received them just this moment. Her empty eye sockets glowing with their ominous light and leaking bloodied puss down her cheeks. She stepped towards me sniffing the air, her bare feet making slapping, sticky sounds with each footfall. I couldn't take my eyes from her and couldn't move. Tears burned my eyes as I realised, I was going to die and then Lola too, but as the Ghastling leaned slowly down over my body, her putrid breath against my cheek, Lola said again, "Lu...?" and the Ghastling shot up and scrabbled towards the sofa and the sound of Lola's voice; moving in jerking, mangled movements as she descended on her prey.

As she left my line of vision my body became my own again and scrabbled across the floor in a desperate attempt to find my knife. The Ghastling was quickly advancing on Lola and I needed to help her, but the knife was nowhere to be found. I reached under the sofa and scurried my fingers around to find it, but it was too far under and I couldn't reach it, would never get it back in time to save Lola. I snarled in frustration and got to my feet as the Ghastling came down on Lola with a ferocious screech that covered the sound of Lola's screams. "Lola hold on, I'm coming!" I yelled as I ran for the Ghastling and threw myself onto her bony grey-skinned back and clawed at her, trying desperately to get her attention from Lola. The Ghastling hissed at me and with a long, slender arm tipped with horribly broken claws knocked me bodily to the ground and the wind huffed out of me.

Lola screamed and I tried to get up but my back throbbed and I was gasping for air. Then before my eyes the Ghastling lifted Lola from the ground by the throat, tore her from neck to navel with her broken claws and began scooping out her insides and devouring them. Lola's body twitched, her breath wheezed as she took her last gasp of air and I vomited at the sight of her intestines hitting the ground. The wet sound of the Ghastling feasting on her kill filled my head and I knew then how futile my attempt was to try and stop her. I struggled to my feet, taking one last look at what was left of Lola, tears blurring my vision and then ran for the open door and for a final chance of safety.

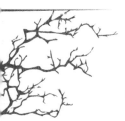

Chapter Eleven

My mind is pretty blank about the details of what came between then and here. Exhaustion, blood loss, fear, trauma and shock had ll taken their toll on me and my mind recalls nothing. I don't know how got from the Ghastling's Hovel to the road, but I've been told often nough that I did, and a driver found me collapsed in the ditch and took ie to hospital. I was in and out of consciousness for a while and spent iuch of my late teens in that hospital bed, once my body was healed, iey feared my mind was still broken and didn't believe a word I told iem. I do remember then coming to me after they searched the ;hastling's Hovel and found the remains of Lola and signs of Teddy, :asey and Mrs Weatherman amongst a few other missing persons whom never knew. They told me I was suspected of the murder of six people, ut that due to my mental instability I was unfit for trial and would pend my remaining days at Posybrooke Mental Institution for Crimi- ally Insane. I remember that part like it was yesterday.

'OU SEE THE THING ABOUT small backwoods villages is, no one elieves in the big bad wolf—it's just a children's story made up to make ttle kids behave and teenagers be wary. It's not real and they won't be- eve it even if it manifests itself and murders a percentage of the vil- ige. They won't believe it unless they see it and everyone who saw it was ead... except me.

It was 1962 when I first met the realities of our little homegrown leg end and lost my friends to the most vile and horrendous of demons. was 1963 when I was locked away for the murder of six people, an accu sation as painful as it is false. It is now 2020 as I write this story for you and I have been stuck in this hellish hole waiting for her to come for m for over 57 years and I am fast approaching the end of my lifespan. Th world will never know that I didn't do those awful things to those poor unfortunate souls and they will never believe that I didn't tear apart m Lola like she meant nothing. I will never have the chance to visit thei graves, to say goodbye or to see my own mother smile at me without th tinges of pain and guilt behind her eyes. The Ghastling has yet to take m soul but she has already destroyed my life completely.

I THOUGHT I HEARD THE woods whispering again last night. but when I woke up, they stopped. I don't know what this means.

I SAW HER TODAY. I'VE been expecting her for over half my life and yet I wasn't prepared to see that unchanged glowing gaze in that gouged and ghoulish face. I was in the garden enjoying some fresh air with book when I felt like I was being watched, I looked around, but no on was paying me much attention and then I saw lights from the corner o my eye. I saw her in the trees beyond iron fencing and my blood ra cold, my bowels turned to fluid and expelled themselves and I jumped up screaming for the nurse to come and look, for anyone to come an see her. Of course, when the Nurse came, the Ghastling had gone an I was just an old woman dripping piss and shit and raving about some thing all but myself considered a delusion. I was roughly cleaned up and told I wouldn't be allowed back outside until I was better able to manage my delusionary episodes, prescribed new brain numbing medication and locked in my room. I sit here now committing my vision to paper, so you know at least that she was there, and I did not imagine her. She's come for me, finally.

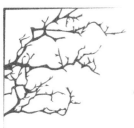

Chapter Twelve

I'm writing this from the Segregation Unit with a green wax crayon because they've taken away my pencils. This morning I saw her again. I had woken late and I wanted a shower, so I collected my things and went to the baths alone. Slinky Steph was in her usual booth, but she paid me no mind as she very seldom leaves her own little world. Once the shower was going at the perfect temperature, I went to the sinks to brush my teeth and as I wiped the condensation from the mirror she was there. My very reflection, staring right into me with those glowing hollowed pits, the Ghastling was in the mirror. I screamed and used the soap dish to smash the mirror to splinters, cutting my hands and fingers to ribbons as I smashed, and smashed, and smashed. When the nurse came running to see what the commotion was, she found me sat in a puddle of blood and glass shards, my hands a wreak, damning her name, "come and get me you bitch, then they'll see your rancid face. Ghastling whore."

My hands are bandaged now and whilst sore they're mostly okay. They don't really hurt, the only thing really hurt is my pride. It's becoming a common thing for the nurses to find me in the most embarrassing states of upset and rage and it's making them think I'm even crazier than they first pegged me. I'm beginning to wonder if that's what she wants them to believe, so that when she takes me, they'll never suspect a thing. Just another loon to lose herself to her violent delusions, no Ghastling, no murder, no worries. Stuff her in the crematory and scatter her to the winds. Clever bitch.

HE'S GETTING CLOSER, I can hear the trees whispering that lulling ıne over and over again in a loop. Just quiet but always there. Letting 1e know the end is near.

HE'S TOYING WITH ME, like a cat batting around a mouse before owly disembowelling it and throwing it aside uneaten. A flicker here, er eyes over there, her face under the bed sheets, but she won't come loser and she's only there for a second, then gone.

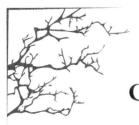

Chapter Thirteen

My time is up and she's finally coming for me. She appeared in th recreation room this evening and I refused to give her the satis faction of another embarrassing episode for her to simply vanish an leave me looking like an old fool so I pointedly ignored her, pretende like I couldn't even see her. What a heartrending mistake that was. I wan dered into the kitchen to get a cup of juice from the drinks counter an came back to the sounds of screaming and crying, nurses frantic and ush ering everyone to their rooms. Lucy and Slinky Steph were torn an bloodied pulps on the ground, blood splattered around the room and th other inmates were wild. A nurse rushed me to my room and locked m in, but I can still hear the screams and cries, can still hear the panickin staff trying to explain the inexplicable to the police as they beg to clea up the mess. I did this. She only hurt them to get to me.

THE BUILDING IS QUIET now and the nurses have all gone still. can't hear even a mouse, but I cannot sleep because she is in here some where and she's waiting for the perfect moment to come for me. I can fee her slinking and skulking around outside the door, but I won't shout ou to her and I won't go to sleep. She won't take me without a fight.

I wonder if something like this has ever happened before and ho the officials deal with such an event. There have only ever been self-in flicted deaths in my 57 years of being at Posybrooke Asylum, but surel somebody somewhere has murdered another inmate, or something un xplainable has happened. The recreation room was full, there were three urses present and two old women seemingly self-combust into showers f blood and guts before their eyes. How would they explain that away ithout being locked in here with us? Will they think of me as they lay errified and shocked in their beds and wonder if maybe I was telling the ruth all along? I have to admit the irony is thrilling.

T'S 3:00AM AND THE trees are singing to me, I was half asleep listening to them when I heard the scratching at the door and the fumbling f the lock. She's out there and she's fed up with waiting. I have no means f escape as I am locked in and I have no means of defending myself as I till have not been allowed pointed objects after the mirror incident—I till write this in wax crayon—and I know that really no weapon would e of use to me anyway. I'm the one that got away and she's taken a long, ong time to savour my torture before coming for me. She thirsts for my ain and suffering as I have thirsted for her end. I can do nothing more han record my last moments for you, so that someone may read my tale nd know that I did not commit those horrible murders, that I was not elusional and that she does exist.

I am Lucinda Porter and I wish that the tale that I have told you was ot my own, sadly it is.

About the Author

KAY PARKER IS AN HISTORIAN and Medievalist from rural Eng
land. Always a lover of the written word, Kay has spent many an hour los
in the pages of all manner of books. She is a keen lover of Sci-fi and Hor
ror fiction. *SLEEPING WITH HER DEMONS* is her first book and
was released in 2020. *THE WHISPERING WOODS* is her second pub
lished work and was written mostly for her mother, but partly for herself

Kay lives with her daughter and their two cats, Mitten and Mist
where when she isn't writing or studying medieval history, she is curled
up with a good book or her SHUDDER subscription.

Still More from Kay Parker
Non-Fiction

Rebellious Women of the Tudor era (Coming Soon from Pen & Sword Books)

Acknowledgements

I would like to thank first and foremost my mother for this one. When I was very young, she introduced me to the world of 80's and 90's horror movies and began my obsession with all things dark. I fondly remember the first time I saw *The Lost Boys, IT (original ver.)* and *Hellraiser.* I also remember the two weeks that I didn't sleep after watching *A Nightmare on Elm Street.* I guess I should thank these movies too, for leaving such a lasting impression on me and still enthralling me today. I'd also like to thank my good friends Abi and Emily who have been so supportive of my writing since the very start when it was all simply a niggling idea, I was too afraid to unpick. I would like to thank M.C. Solaris for her unbridled support in my work even when it scares the socks off of her. I'd like to thank my sister Chantelle and brother-in-law for vowing to read anything I write and making me laugh when they tell me about their nightly reading sessions of my work. I'd like to thank my late grandmother who set a love of reading in me so deeply that I couldn't shake it if I tried and for always being there when I couldn't turn to anyone else. Special mentions to @wolfba3, Emma @haunting.reads and T @Treadstosurvive for championing this book and being so enthusiastic about it. I'd like to thank everyone who's given a kind word and shared enthusiasm for my work and especially I'd like to thank my family for making endless mugs of tea and amusing my daughter whilst I got these words from my skull and into these pages. I love you all. Don't let the Ghastling get you.

Kay xo

...

Printed in Great Britain
by Amazon

60501923R00031